Trevor

Mustafa Kulle

Acknowledgements

Special Thanks to my Editor Dr. Stephen Carver

Special Thanks to my family and friends for all their love and support.

A man spat on the wet pavement as he pushed past teenaged Trevor. The spit dissolved into the puddle in the cracks of the slabs while the rest wobbled upon each tread. They've been cracking up for years but the council never bothered to replace them. As Trevor walked on with his hooded head facing down, he kept a brief mental record of the things he saw on his way. Cigarette butts scattered, flattened chewing gum, pieces of an old printer tossed to the side, crushed empty drink cans... and then he spotted the patch of blood that someone forgot to clean off. It was the result of a stabbing the night before. But which one was it? Hard to tell when these things occur all the time. Trevor tried to recall the victims he heard about recently. Perhaps the victim was the Somali immigrant after he stepped out of the job centre across the road? Or was it the Turkish teenager who refused to give up his phone? Who cares? Nobody he knew anyway. "Shit happens", he thought.

Police sirens echoed from the distance. Night and day, there was no end to them. So far no sound of a fire engine or an ambulance... yet. Crime was the norm here.

It had been raining all day and it stopped about an hour ago. Each step he took made his feet wet, there were holes in his trainers. This urban area would have been pitch black if it weren't for the dim amber street lights illuminating it. Every other bulb flickered.

As he walked, he heard a group of drunken men standing outside a pub, they sang loud football anthems out of tune, belched in between, and then laughed like wild hyenas. It had already passed closing time.

Another person was holding onto a lamp post while vomiting into the gutter of the road. The yellow substance trailed along as it dissolved into the rainwater before going down into the sewer.

Then he heard a drunk couple fucking in a dark dirty alleyway.

When the world around Trevor got his attention, he noticed the new graffiti sprayed on top of the older ones that were fading. At least that looked better. All the buildings were crumbling due to years of little to no maintenance by the government. They have been darkened by pollution and acid rain. Green moss were spreading across each wet surface.

The sound of a brick being thrown through a car window made Trevor jump. The car emitted its screeching alarm as if crying for help while a gang of black teenagers kicked it and smacked it with baseball bats. Another member poured some sort of liquid inside, took out a lighter and then set it on fire. The whole interior was aflame. The boys danced around with excitement as they filmed the whole thing with their smart phones. Soon the fire covered the entire vehicle. It looked like it was going to explode. The boys scattered as they cheered with delight. Trevor figured it was probably another dare out of boredom. It was matter of time before someone called the fire brigade. That is, if anyone was bothered. Since their parents didn't want them playing video games, "go outside" they said, "get some fresh air" they said. Well, there was nothing to do out here. Fuck it. Just do whatever.

It's a dark world. Dark things happen here. This was Trevor's home. One of the worst areas of London.

Trevor walked on. He took in a deep breath before he coughed it back out. The air reeked of a cocktail of odours; smoke from kebab shops working late at night, waste filled to the brims of the bins outside fast food restaurants, litter spilled everywhere. Among them was a tramp scavenging for food.

Trevor's nose was bleeding from snorting cocaine earlier. There were still traces of the white powder around his nostrils. His heart beat raced as though he'd been sprinting. On the surface he looked steady, but his hands were shaky. He was looking for a place to rob. He tried to remember which ones he hadn't yet broken into. So far, he only burgled houses. He thought he'd better not leave a pattern. So he headed for the council houses.

He went over to a block of flats. As he climbed up the outdoor staircase, each landing had an overhanging smell of urine in the air.

He settled for the third floor not knowing why. He walked down the hallway. The place was made of dirty concrete slabs. Every other flat he walked passed had its own muffled cacophony of noises: A family was heard arguing in some foreign language, while another had its television on full blast. Of course. Why not. Fuck the neighbours. The rest were quiet.

He made his way towards the end of the hallway where

there was a window that had no blind. It was dark inside. He looked in, the coast was clear. He checked the kitchen window. It was weak at the frames. He looked around. There was no one in sight. He took out his crowbar, carefully wedged it between the gaps, pulled hard until the window was opened. He climbed in.

He looked around and there was nothing that caught his attention. Nothing worth stealing. Although he was indoors, he felt cold, his hands were shaking and his breathing was unsteady. He felt tense, agitated. As he searched the flat he accidentally knocked an ornament on to the floor and it smashed.

"Shit!" He exclaimed and tried to make a run for the window. A tall man immediately confronted him and turned on the light. He filled the door frame.

"Oi! What are you doin' here?!"

"Gimme yer money..." Trevor took out the crowbar "and I'll go."

"Right! Come here!" The man attempted to challenge Trevor, for he was bigger than him. Trevor panicked. Holding the crowbar tightly with both hands, he swung at the man's neck, the hook of the crowbar jammed instantly at the man's neck. The man was choking, looking into Trevor's eyes the most frightening look he had ever seen. Blood was coming out of the man's neck and mouth, his hands were clenched on to the crowbar trying to pull it out, while Trevor tried to yank it out, it wouldn't budge. The struggle was too much for Trevor to bear, he lost his balance and the man fell on top of him. Trevor pushed the man off while still trying to get the crowbar out of his neck, choking to death on his blood. Trevor stumbled to his feet, a woman ran into the room and started to scream.

"Shut up! Shut up!" Trevor shouted. He was blinded with panic. He grabbed the crowbar one last time with both hands and yanked it out of the man's neck. The man's arm dropped to the floor. The woman tried to run to the front door, Trevor caught up quickly and hit her in the back with the crowbar. The woman fell on the floor. She turned around to face her tormentor;

"Get out!" she screamed. Trevor hit her on the head with the crowbar. She screamed louder, as she tried to gouge Trevor's eyes with her nails. Trevor punched her in the face and then hit her on the head with the crowbar and again and again. "Shut up!" he shouted one last time. The woman fell silent and suddenly became still. Trevor whispered "I told you to shut up, didn't I."

At this point, Trevor was weak, he let go of the crowbar, slowly rose to his feet and leaned against the wall.

Breathing heavily, he tried to comprehend what he had done. His heart was pounding so hard and loud he could hear it. He looked at the woman lying on the floor with her head in a pool of blood. He couldn't bear the sight of her deformed terrorised face, so he looked the other way and he saw the man lying on the floor, also in a pool of blood, coming from his neck. Trevor became afraid. Frightened. He didn't know what to do. Panting, and scared, he tried to think. The drugs had taken their toll, all he could think of was escape. He pushed himself away from the wall, picked up the crowbar, and put it under his coat.

Just as he was about to make his way into the kitchen

where the open window was, he heard the sound of a crying baby. He stopped and froze on the spot. He became afraid again. But instead of continuing his escape, his feet followed the sound; he gently pushed the door open, and turned on the light. He saw a baby girl crying in her cot. The room was pink with white hearts all over the walls. The room was full of baby toys, this was the little girl's bedroom; the cot had lit shapes spiralling on its mobile as it turned, the cupboards had stickers of Disney Princesses, shelves of toddler books and lots of teddy bears everywhere.

This was an alien world to Trevor. He had never seen anything like this. He never had his own room or anything to play with, unless it was something Auntie Katherine gave him on rare occasions.

Then he turned to the baby girl, still crying and in need of attention.

His jaw trembled. Tears began to fill his eyes. He gulped. He was about to wipe his eyes until he saw what the light revealed. There was blood on his hands. He looked with dismay. The strong smell made him feel sick. He began to cry.

"What... have... I... done?"

A loud thunder cracked outside, the heavy rain returned. The sound brought Trevor back to his senses. Racked with guilt, full of sorrow, he picked her up, wrapped her up in her warm blanket and held her in his arms. Just before he left, he saw a teddy bear in her bed holding a heart. On the heart it read 'Samantha'.

"Ok Samantha…" he whispered to her, upon which she became silent "listen to me, I need you to do me big favour. Just keep quiet." The baby somehow understood, and obeyed.

Trevor left the room and made his way into the kitchen, climbed out of the window and then ran with the baby in his arms.

He climbed down the stairs, made his way down the street and ran as fast as he could. The sound of police sirens were accompanied by fire engines. He stepped on a used condom beside a dark alleyway as he ran. There was nobody on the streets. The rain made everyone disperse. It was only Trevor and baby Samantha in the rain.

He ran to the train station to catch the next train to Hull, hoping to find Auntie Katherine and a place to stay. By the time he got to Hull it was morning, he was cold and the girl was hungry and crying. He needed to find Aunt Katherine fast.

As he searched the streets of Hull, it was pouring with rain, freezing cold as the wind blew the water onto his face, soaking his clothes and could no longer keep Samantha dry. They were cold, drenched and tired. The cold made Trevor's hands tremble, his fingers and toes felt like they were frost bitten. He was worried for Samantha for she was now crying in his arms.

Eventually, he found Aunt Katherine's house, reached for the front door and knocked on it. Upon opening the door, Katherine had the biggest surprise of her life. No one in her family ever came to visit her from London, nor did she ever expect anyone at such an hour, not even Trevor, to come all this way to see her.

"Trevor?! What on earth are you doing here?" She gasped. "Aunt Katherine, my baby is hungry."

■

Trevor stayed with Aunt Katherine and kept his whereabouts a secret and didn't contact anybody. They kept themselves to themselves, keeping a low profile. With Katherine's guidance, Trevor raised Samantha as his own. Eventually he found himself a job, first working in a shop stacking shelves, then as a marketing consultant. Trevor did his best for Samantha. He gave up everything for her and for the first time in his life, he put the needs of someone else before himself. He took counselling sessions and sought therapy for his drug addiction. All he ever thought about was Samantha. Always putting her before himself. He felt he owed her everything.

As the years passed, Trevor transformed into a man he never imagined himself to be. Samantha grew up to be a beautiful girl. Samantha loved Trevor dearly. Thinking he was her own father. It had been 17 years after Trevor brought Samantha to Hull. Katherine fell ill and there was no saving her. In time she became bed ridden. She was going to die soon.

In her deathbed, before she died, Katherine called Trevor over to her; she looked into his eyes more sternly than ever, and whispered,

"Promise me you'll tell her."

Trevor froze and became afraid. He could not believe she could make such a request just when she was about to leave this world. He felt trapped and helpless. He couldn't blink, his heart was pounding and he swallowed hard. Tears began to fill his eyes and run down his cheeks, trying not to cry, struggling to breathe.

She was the only person who was there for him. She was his only family, anyone else would have turned a blind eye and deserted him. But Katherine, was a saint to him. She had been a mother, an auntie to him, and a grandmother to Samantha. This was not the time to let her down. He has enough guilt as it is, the last thing he needed was the burden of not keeping a promise. He nodded reluctantly yet she knew he meant his agreement.

Months after Aunt Katherine passed away, it was Samantha's 18th birthday. The day went as normal, one early afternoon when she came home with her boyfriend Stephen for lunch. They were a happy couple. She opened the door, nobody was in, and proceeded to putting the kettle on. As Stephen made his way to the lounge, he spotted an envelope with 'Samantha' written on it.

"Hey look, you have a card." He gleefully said as he sat on the couch.

"Oh gosh, he's never done this before." She came in. A little surprised, she smiled.

"Must be a big surprise" He smiled.

She opened the envelope, and pulled out a letter, it was

two pages long and handwritten. Her happy face turned confused, then puzzled, then ...shock. She stood frozen.

"What's the matter?" Stephen enquired.

Silence.

He got up from his seat and walked over to her.
"Sammy, are you alright?

More silence.

As he was about to lean in she jerked the letter away, ran into the kitchen and hastily grabbed her bag.

"I have to go to London. Now! I can't explain. I don't know. I have to do this, I'll tell you everything as soon as I can."

"What's going on? Why are you being so —"?

"Stephen please, I need you to take me to the station right now. I've got to go to London."

Understanding the urgency, Stephen rushed to the door and took out his car key,

"Can I come with you?" He asked.

"No, this is something I have to do on my own."

She took the next train to London with the letter, in her hands, reading it over and over

Trying to comprehend everything, her head was spinning.

At the bottom of the letter, it had the address of where she used to live. Using her smart phone, she knew exactly where to go once she reached London.

Trevor was in the flat where it all began. It was empty, and uninhabited since that day. But it didn't stop looters from crashing in and squatters sleeping over. After all these years, the council never bothered to get it inspected, refurbished, or cleaned up for someone else to move in. Of course, even if there were new occupants, no way they could live there knowing that people had been murdered there. They would hear about it from the locals.

Trevor was distraught. Weak. This guilt he wanted no more.

Over and over, he was going through the whole ordeal in his head. He remembered where everything was. The kitchen window, the ornament that smashed, everything he could remember.

He looked for traces of blood but the laminated flooring was torn out. He often wondered what it was that broke. Had he not knocked it over all those years ago, he probably would have just taken something random and left.

The more he looked, the more agitated and annoyed he became, he was hoping to find something but he wasn't sure what though. There was nothing in the flat to indicate his presence. No traces of blood or anything of the sort. It was all in his head. Playing on loop like a broken record.

The flat looked nothing like the way it was, with the wallpaper stripped, carpet removed, faded colours and paint peeling. The stench of cigarettes and drugs lingered in the air. But there was nothing in this flat that could distract him from the horrible images in his head.

Among the floorboards, he found an old newspaper. He picked it up and he was instantly frightened.

The headline read: 'Local Family Murdered'.

He began to feel sick, but he continued to read the article, which continued into the centre pages. It was big news. The photos horrified him. It showed the man on the floor with a blanket covering his face, and another photo, of the woman, also with her face covered. This brought it all back, everything became crystal clear. Only he knew what was under those blankets. He remembered their faces when he killed them, and the sounds they made in their last moments. Then finally, there was a photo of the empty cot. That moment made him gag.

He pulled himself away for a moment to steady himself before he continued to read.

The newspaper was full of the crudest journalism; making speculations about whether it was a gang or a drug related incident, rather than a robbery gone wrong.

A mixture of so-called eyewitness accounts claiming they saw an immigrant and assuming the suspect was a black male. Speculations from so-called experts and politicians with their opinions were added. Then it was followed by comments from readers, making foul remarks and making fun of the whole situation like it was some sort of a joke.

All this could have been funny if wasn't so disgusting.

Infuriated by the crude wording and the lame guesswork, he knew too well what the truth was. This piece of crap he had in his hand was nothing but entertainment for the masses. Doing his best to contain himself, he closed his eyes, folded the newspaper and threw it aside as he left the room.

He made his way into Samantha's old bedroom where the cot was, only there was none. The room was completely bare. The pink wallpaper with the white hearts was no longer there; the walls were soggy and damp. No shelf with children's books. No teddy bears.

He could hear the crying in his head as he imagined the cot in the very spot of the room he looked at. He looked up and he saw wire coming down from the ceiling. He sighed.

He reached into his coat pocket and pulled a long Ethernet cable, which he made into a noose. All he had to do was attach it to the ceiling. And that would be the end of it. He planned for Samantha to find him dead. Perhaps it's what Samantha would have wanted. There was no better place or state to find him in. This would be his punishment.

He was just about to finish tightening the wires when the bedroom door was flung open. It was Samantha.

"Trevor?!" She cried. Trevor was caught off guard, it was too late. He didn't know what to say. "Don't even think about it!" she bellowed as she ran over and shoved him into the other side of the room so hard, his back hit the wall.

"You bastard!" She shouted and slapped him around

the face repeatedly, hitting him until he fell to the floor, opening himself up to all the punishment that was waiting for him.

She turned around to recollect herself, she stood in the middle of the room, with her face in her hands and wept as the noose was hanging above her head, slowly swinging from side to side, turning in a spiral motion just like the way her mobile did when she was a baby. Things have come full circle.

Trevor was on the floor, weakened by the episode. He too began to cry. He was in no position for a fight, this was it. It was time to face his judge, jury and executioner. And that was Samantha. He bowed his head completely.

"Oh my god I can't believe you," she wiped her tears. As she turned to face Trevor, "And to find that you were about to..." she looked at the noose. "No! No!" She yelled as she yanked the wires from the ceiling with all her raging strength and threw it across the room.

Distraught, she panted. She tried to recollect herself as she cried. She then began to breathe slowly as she stood up straight. She tightened her fists, gritted her teeth behind her firm lips. She cleared her throat. And at last she spoke.

"You are not going anywhere. I will never forgive you until I know everything. You understand."

Trevor slowly shook his head feebly and could not control his tears.

"Samantha, I couldn't tell you. I just couldn't. I didn't

want to see you like this. I would have thought you wanted me dead after I told you."

"No. Do you not understand? That would have made everything worse. You were going to leave me with unanswered questions only to spend the rest of my life wondering what else you've been hiding."

Trevor slowly sat up with his back against the wall and looked up at Samantha standing over him.

"That's all there is to it. I was so stupid. It was a terrible mistake I wish I never did. I couldn't change what happened. I thought I could make it up to you by looking after you. Raising you as my own."

She paused. "Did Katherine know?"

"Yes. She knew I couldn't live this lie forever, and she was right. I promised her I'd tell you. When I first told her, she was going to call the police. But then she thought about you. What would happen to you? Adoption? Foster care? And since it was your life I had ruined, I had to pay the price. Also, she couldn't have children you see. She was divorced. She always wanted to have children. You could say she raised us both. Pretty much."

Samantha began to feel weak too, she stumbled towards the opposite wall and sat down.

"But, why this place? What were you doing here...you know...when it happened?" She asked.

"When I broke into your parents' home, I was looking for something to steal, I was so hooked on drugs that I needed money. I wasn't thinking straight. That's what drugs do to you. They devastate lives, as it did my parents, me, and then your family. All this is the result of it." Trevor explained.

She smacked her lips and nodded.

"So that's why you had a strict stance on drugs this whole time. Now it's clear why you were sceptical of all my friends, going out was a hassle thanks to you. It was so difficult to convince you to let me go to a party."

"Yes. I made sure you never fell into the same pit as I did because I knew the effects far too well." He looked around the room then continued. "If I left you, they would have put you into care, not that anybody in those establishments knew what the word 'care' meant. They would have neglected you. The same way my parents neglected me. Taking you in, as mine was the right decision I made. I have lived with this guilt since that day. I never thought you could ever forgive me. I grew to love you so much I couldn't bear to look at you... to see you hurt in such a way."

Trevor was beginning to cry again.

"So that's why it was easier for me to just kill myself."

Trevor broke down. His hands covered his face and wept. Samantha watched as she slowly shook her head.

"No one ever loved me. Nobody cared about me. Ever. The only person who did was Aunt Katherine." He sobbed. "The world I knew was cruel, heartless."

He sniffed, wiped his tears, got up, walked over to the window and looked outside. Samantha too stood up, walked slowly towards his side and looked.

"This is the place I grew up in," He explained.

Police sirens could be heard. On the streets down below, he saw a drunk man, struggling to walk in a straight line. Across the dirty street, a gang of black men were fighting each other. Further down the street there was group of neighbours, shouting at each other, swearing and hurling verbal abuse at the top of their voices while young children stood by and watched.

"It's disgusting", she commented.

"I could not raise you in a place like this. I heard it was quieter up north. Well, it's certainly better to be out of the city."

He turned away from the window and faced the door.

"Well, Samantha, I guess that's everything. I have nothing else to say. So what happens now? Do you want me to walk out your life for good? You going to call the police?"

"No. I told you. You are not going anywhere. Especially when I need a family, right now. You're all the family I've got." She tried to be strong and put on a brave face. "I need you. I'm pregnant."

"Is it..." Trevor was about to ask.

"Yes, it's Stephen's." Samantha cut him. There was a silent pause. "He proposed, and I said yes."

"Samantha… I'm sorry." Trevor was overwhelmed by all the good news at the most unexpected circumstances.

"Don't be like that. Now do you understand? I need a Dad. I need you to walk me down the aisle. I need you to be there for my baby and be a Granddad."

"Oh Samantha, I will," Trevor responded with more sentiment than ever. Tears filled his eyes again.
"Just promise me you'll never walk out on me ever again." She said sternly.

"I won't. I swear, I will take care of you for the rest of my life. I promise."

They embraced and held each other tightly and sobbed. Never in his life had Trevor imagined he would ever have such emotions racing through him like this.

■

Trevor and Samantha spent the night at the local Bed and Breakfast. Samantha called Stephen and told him that everything was okay and she's with her Dad in London and they'll return soon. The next day, they went to find the gravestones of Samantha's parents.

And there they were, one marble gravestone with two photos. One of Sarah Young, and one of Peter Young. Both were smiling. Looking at the marble gravestone, it's clean and has been well looked after by the locals. They were respected members of the community. Samantha, knelt down to lay her flowers. Afterwards they stood there, Trevor and Samantha held each other as they looked on.

Samantha always knew herself as Samantha James, but having learned her real surname, it didn't matter because she was going to get married to Stephen soon and it was time to move on.

Samantha took Trevor by the arm.

"Come on, Dad. Let's go home" She lead him to the train station, together they returned to Hull to start their lives afresh.

The End.